Rachel, a Hutterite Girl

Library of Congress Cataloging-in-Publication Data

Maendel, Rachel, 1937-
    Rachel, a Hutterite girl / Rachel Maendel : illustrated by Hannah Marsden.
        p. cm.
    Summary: Rachel, a young girl who lives on a big farm with other Hutterite families, sleeps in a Schlobonk bed, visits Uncle Jacob's shoe shop, and watches a hen hatch a nest of goose eggs.
        ISBN 0-8361-9119-6 (alk. paper)
        [1. Hutterite Brethren Fiction. 2. Farm life Fiction.]
    I. Marsden, Hannah, 1946-   ill. II. Title.
    PZ7.M2669Rac   1999
    [E]—dc21   99-29922

RACHEL, A HUTTERITE GIRL
Copyright © 1999 by Herald Press, Harrisonburg, Va. 15683
    Published simultaneously in Canada by Herald Press, Kitchener, Ont. N2L 6H7.
    All rights reserved
Library of Congress Catalog Card Number: 99-29922
International Standard Book Number: 0-8361-9119-6
Printed in the United States of America
Book design by Gwen M. Stamm

08 07 06 05 04   10 9 8 7 6 5 4 3

To order or request information,
please call 1-800-759-4447 (individuals);
1-800-245-7894 (trade).
Website: www.heraldpress.com

Rachel, a Hutterite Girl

Rachel Maendel

Illustrated by Hannah Marsden

Herald Press

Harrisonburg, Virginia
Kitchener, Ontario

Dedicated to my parents,

John and Sarah Maendel,

to whom I owe my happy childhood.

Rachel was a little Hutterite girl.

She lived on a big farm, with many Hutterite families.

She didn't have a television.

She didn't have a bicycle.

She didn't have books to read
or dishes for her dolls.

But Rachel was a happy girl. She had parents who loved her. Voter told
her stories and taught her to be kind. Mueter sewed her clothes, and
knitted her socks and mittens.

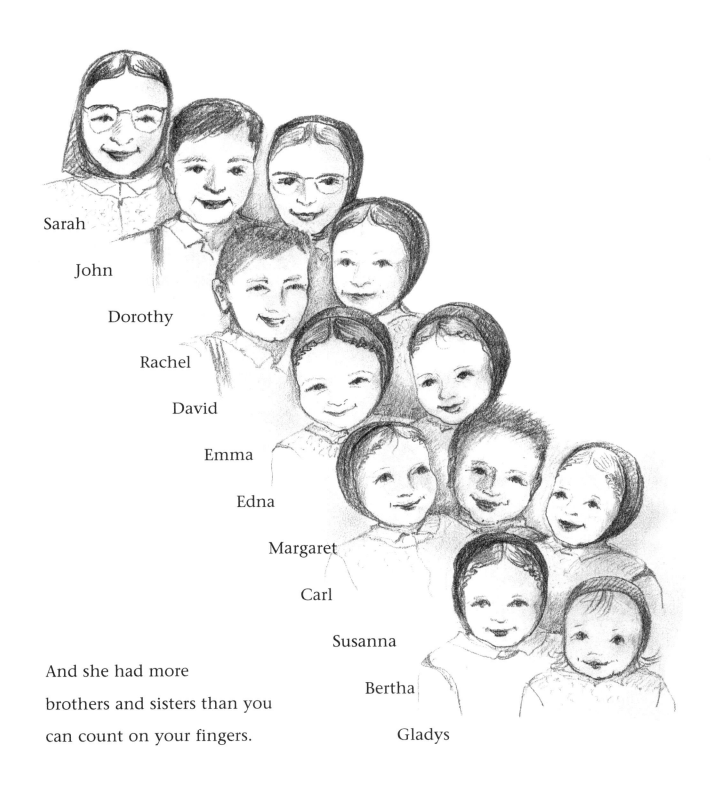

Sarah

John

Dorothy

Rachel

David

Emma

Edna

Margaret

Carl

Susanna

Bertha

Gladys

And she had more
brothers and sisters than you
can count on your fingers.

She had more aunties and uncles than you can count
on your fingers and toes, your ears, and your nose.

Jacob   *David*   *Johannes*   *Josh*   *Rebecca*   *Kalep*

    Sarah   *Rachel*   *Katie*   *Susie*   *Susanna*   *Joe*

Rachel   Jacob   Annie   Susanna   Paul   Joe   Johannes

   Elisebeth   Sarah   Mike   Katerina   Mary

And she had two sets of grandparents, named for the farm colonies where they lived,

Elm River Ol Vetter and Ankela   James Valley Ol Vetter and Ankela

and oodles and oodles of cousins.

There was always
a baby in Rachel's
family, and Aunt
Rachel would come
to look after Mueter
and the new little one.
Then she would light the wood stove, even in the summer, to heat water
for the baby's bath and for washing diapers.

"Come, Rachel," Aunt Rachel would say. "You can help me bathe
the baby in the little wooden tub."

When the baby was dry, Aunt Rachel would rub goose fat all over the
baby's pink skin and make her look shiny.

How Rachel loved to hear the baby's happy noises! Mueter called it
jubling.

One spring morning, Rachel woke up in her *Schlofbonk* bed, beside her sister Dorothy. She could hear Mueter and Voter singing praise songs, as they did every day. The tunes they sang were slow and solemn, but Rachel loved to hear them sing together.

Outside, the morning was cold, but Rachel and Dorothy could feel warmth coming from the stovepipe in their room. It was attached to the wood stove down in the living room. The other rooms had stovepipes to heat them, too. Voter started the fire each morning, with wood that he and the uncles and big cousins had chopped in the woods nearby. When he cleaned out the stove, he saved the ashes for Mueter to soften the water for the next laundry day.

Rachel and Dorothy jumped out of bed and got dressed quickly. Their skirts went way down to their shoes, and they put aprons on top. An apron was so handy! You could use it to wipe spills and carry things. You could keep your hands warm when you forgot your mittens, and you could even use it as a hanky. Before Rachel was five, she wore a bib apron, but now that she was older, she wore a half-apron. Her dress closed down the front with hooks and eyes instead of buttons.

"We don't use buttons because soldiers use them," Voter said.

After they were dressed, Rachel and Dorothy tidied up their room. As they folded the big feather bed, Rachel thought about the times they helped with *Feder schleissen*, pulling soft feathers off the quills to make a feather bed. Cousin Katie and Cousin Sarah always told wonderful stories as they worked!

Now Rachel and Dorothy pushed in the front of the *Schlofbonk*, unhooked the leather strap, and carefully let down the lid. During the day, the *Schlofbonk* became a *Ruabonk*, to sit on.

The girls hurried downstairs to wash their hands and faces at the washstand in the little *Gangle*. They flipped the washbowl down from the wall and poured hot water into it from the big pot on the stove. It was the boys' job to keep the pot filled with water.

The slippery, homemade soap was white in Rachel's hand. It was hard to believe that Mueter and Uncle Paul had made it from horrid-smelling, leftover fat.

"Rachel, take the bucket of milk out to the refrigerator, will you?"
Mueter called.

Rachel took the bucket and the girls went outside. The refrigerator was
a covered hole in the ground, by the steps. When Rachel opened the lid,
she screamed and jumped. A big, black lizard was looking up at her!

Dorothy chased the lizard away so Rachel could put the bucket of milk down in the dark hole, where it would stay cool.

"Hurry, Rachel," she urged. "We'll be late for breakfast." Hand in hand, the girls ran to the *Essenschul*, where they would eat breakfast with the other colony children.

When they got there, the big room was already full of children. They sat quietly at the tables, in order of age. The boys sat on one side of the room and the girls on the other. The German schoolteacher and Aunt Susie were there to serve breakfast. Today they were having roasted barley coffee, along with the usual homemade bread, butter, and fresh honey.

When breakfast was over, Dorothy had to wash dishes with the older girls, but Rachel skipped out to the pig barn with her cousin, Rebecca. The first thing they did was climb into the hayloft. They burrowed into the hay to make comfortable, soft seats.

"Remember last week? Your little brother Carl hid here all day long because he was scared of the dentist," giggled Rebecca.

"I was scared too when the dentist came around," said Rachel, "but it didn't hurt that much to have my wiggly tooth pulled." She felt the rough edge of her new tooth with her tongue.

Secretly, she was glad the dentist hardly ever came to the colony.

"Let's go see the baby pigs," said Rebecca.

The girls climbed down the ladder again. Only the shiny, pink piglets were in the barn, because the mother sows were out in the yard. The baby pigs' skin was smooth and soft as satin, and they had cute, curly tails. They squealed and squealed, running round and round the pen when Rachel and Rebecca tried to catch them.

"Uh-oh, look at your shoes," said Rebecca, pointing to Rachel's feet. "They're all muddy."

"Oh dear, what will Mueter say?" worried Rachel.

"Let's run to Uncle Jacob's shoe shop and clean them," said Rebecca.

They ran across the yard to the shoe shop and found a brush and a tin of oil right by the door. Carefully, the girls wiped off their shoes with some hay, dipped the thick brush into the oil, and brushed their shoes. Now the leather was soft and shiny.

They pushed open the shop door and smelled the strong smell of glue and leather.

Rachel loved visiting Uncle Jacob's shop. Finished shoes stood on the shelves, all ready for children and grown-ups in the colony. Rachel and Rebecca wondered which ones would be their own shoes this fall.

Uncle Jacob stood behind his workbench, hammering on an upside-down shoe. He couldn't talk, because his mouth was full of little tacks. When he needed a tack, he pushed it out of his mouth with his tongue, grabbed it with his fingers, and hammered it into the shoe.

When Uncle Jacob was done hammering and could talk, he took a little pair of buckle shoes from the shelf behind him. "Here, girls, take these shoes to Rachel's mother, for the baby."

The girls skipped down the path to Rachel's house, carrying the pair of tiny new shoes. When they passed the river, they searched for eggs among the rushes and grasses on the shore. The geese liked to hide their nests there. Sure enough, they found several secret nests with eggs. Carefully, Rachel and Rebecca put the eggs in their aprons to carry home.

When they reached the house, Mueter and Aunt Susie were talking in the living room. Mueter was so happy for the pair of little shoes!

"What do you girls have in your aprons?" Aunt Susie asked.

"Eggs!" they said, proudly.

"My, those birds are early layers!" exclaimed Mueter.

"You must find a broody hen and

put those goose eggs under her," Aunt Susie told them, "then they'll hatch. You can tell a broody hen by the rumbly noises she makes, and if her legs have turned yellow."

"Let's go right now to the chicken barn and see if we can find a broody hen!" cried Rebecca. The two girls put the goose eggs in a warm place and ran all the way to the chicken barn.

Pete Hofer was there, gathering eggs. "You may have a broody hen if you find one," said Pete. "But first you must help me collect the eggs."

Rachel and Rebecca worked hard, running up and down in front of the chicken nests, gathering eggs. The eggs felt warm and smooth in Rachel's hands. She thought they were beautiful. The hens were proud of them too and cackled noisily.

By the end of the morning, the girls had found a little brown hen that looked and sounded broody, just as Aunt Susie had said. The little hen was ready to sit on a nest of eggs and raise a family.

Carefully, Rachel and Rebecca carried the little hen home, bringing some straw for a nest.

"Can Voter make a box for my little brown hen?" Rachel asked.

"Maybe after dinner, when he comes home," said Mueter.

"But what if he doesn't hear the dinner bell?" Rachel wondered anxiously.

"Well, if he doesn't," Mueter teased, "Uncle John will have to climb the ladder in the grain elevator and wave his hanky through the little window at the top. Ol Vetter used to do that, when no one had a pocket watch, to let the men know it was dinnertime. When they saw the white hanky, they knew it was time.

"I'm sure Voter will get here for dinner," she added, with a smile.

There were *Nookela* (dumplings) for dinner, made with lots of eggs and flour. Everyone loved them, but Rachel could hardly wait for the meal to be over.

She hurried outside and found Voter lying in the grass under the trees, for *Mittogstund* (midday rest time). "I have a broody hen and some eggs," she told him proudly. Then she asked Voter if he could make her a nest box. "I already have the straw here in my apron."

Voter got up slowly from his rest. He took Rachel by the hand, and together they walked to the carpentry shop. They built a small box from wood and set it under a tree next to the house. Now the little hen had a cozy house. Rachel didn't forget to give her some grain to eat, and some water from the rain barrel at the corner of the house.

Every day Rachel took good care of her little hen and checked the eggs to be sure they were all right. The days grew warmer, and spring was turning into summer. But time moved so slowly for Rachel. It seemed that those eggs would never hatch! Sometimes during *Mittogstund*, Rachel would just lie in the grass, watching the little brown hen that sat patiently, day after day, fluffed up in her box.

One day Rebecca came to play, and Rachel was glad because it made the time go faster. They played with the rag dolls they had made from scraps of material, without using a needle and thread. The girls loved their plain little dolls, and they had so much fun, they forgot to be quiet.

"Shh!" called Mueter. "You're being too noisy. If you girls will be quiet, you can come to the cow barn this afternoon. We're making ice cream."

Mmmm, ice cream! Rachel loved ice cream, but she was a little bit scared of the cow barn. Mueter got up early every morning to help milk the cows, so she was used to them. But the 20 gentle Holstein cows sounded so sad to Rachel, as they lowed and bellowed with their big eyes rolling. She was sure they missed their calves, which were kept in a separate pen.

She knew that Uncle Paul was taking good care of the calves, though, letting them drink as much milk as they wanted from a bucket. How they slurped and sucked as they dipped their faces deep into the frothy milk!

When Rachel and Rebecca reached the cow barn, other colony girls were already in the milk house, eagerly watching the women make ice cream.

The cream, eggs, sugar, and vanilla were closed in the ice cream container with crushed ice and salt water packed around the outside. A dasher stirred the mixture constantly to keep the ice cream soft as it froze. As the cream thickened, the dasher moved more and more slowly. Finally, it stopped.

"Now you may lick the dasher," Aunt Liz called. This was what the children were waiting for! The ice cream smelled so sweet and good, and it tasted so delicious.

"How is the little brown hen, Rachel?" asked Aunt Sarah, after a while.

"Oh, no! I haven't fed and watered her today!" Rachel cried in dismay, ice cream dripping from her chin.

"Can we go and see her?" asked the other children eagerly.

"Only if you're very, very quiet," said Rachel. The girls left the barn to visit the broody hen.

The little brown hen clucked and pecked at the grain Rachel had brought. The children crowded around and stared in wonder at the nest of goose eggs.

"I need to test the eggs," said Rachel, "to see if they're still good."

Rebecca ran to get a bucket of warm water from the kitchen. The little brown hen clucked nervously as Rachel carefully dropped each of her eggs into the warm water. The children watched the eggs twitch and wiggle, then float upright to the top of the water. Only one egg sank to the bottom. That meant it was no good.

"Let me have that one!" called John, Rachel's brother. He was four years older than Rachel and had just finished his barn chores.

He took the egg and threw it against a tree. What a bang it made! It smelled terrible, and the children held their noses and burst out laughing.

"I wish I had a nest of eggs," said Eva, looking wistfully at the little hen sitting safely on the eggs again.

"So do I," said Mary.

"Me too," said Elisabeth.

"Well, let's go down to the river and see if we can find some," said Rachel.

"Yes! A good idea!" they all chorused.

The girls ran down to the river, with Rachel proudly leading the way. They looked and looked among the tall reeds but found no eggs.

Rachel didn't want the others to be disappointed. "Let's go berry picking instead," she said. "I know where there are wild raspberries on the other side of the clearing."

"But we're not allowed to cross the fence," said little Emma.

Rachel didn't pay any attention. She led the children farther and farther away from the colony.

On the far side of the meadow, they found lots of raspberry bushes, but the berries were still green. They searched and searched, but couldn't find even one ripe berry. Suddenly the girls found themselves in the middle of a herd of beef cattle. The cattle had wandered up while they were busy eating. In the center of the herd stood the bull with a ring in his nose, pawing the ground and tossing his head. He was coming closer and closer.

"Help! The bull's going to charge at us!" someone shouted. Terrified, the children ran for their lives to a little hay shed at the edge of the field.

They dashed in, slammed the door, and bolted it tight. The bull had followed them and was snorting angrily outside. The children peeked through the cracks of the boards, wondering what to do next.

"We're going to be late for supper!" wailed Rebecca.

"It's already getting dark," cried Eva. "How will we get home?"

Some of the younger children began to cry softly. The shadows lengthened as the sun sank lower in the sky, and the children were still trapped in the shed.

We'll never get home, and it's all my fault, Rachel thought guiltily.

All of a sudden, they heard the "yap, yap, yap" of a little dog. It was Fido, Pete Hofer's scruffy little dog that always liked to follow the children. Rachel was afraid of Fido, because he showed his sharp teeth when he barked. But now she was glad to see him.

The girls watched breathlessly as Fido ran at the bull. The bull lowered his head to charge with his horns. He snorted and turned, lashing his tail, as Fido jumped out of reach. Each time the bull charged, Fido darted away, running farther and farther from the shed.

Finally, the dog and the bull were at the far end of the field. The girls opened the door quickly, ran across the meadow, and scrambled under the fence. Fido ran to meet them, barking and jumping. He wagged his tail furiously and tried to lick their faces.

"Good dog!" said Rebecca. "Hooray for Fido!"

Happy and tired, the children walked home as fast as they could. They didn't tell anyone what had happened.

One morning the bright sun woke Rachel early. She ran downstairs and hurried to the little brown hen's box. The hen was clucking happily with her feathers fluffed out over her nest.

Rachel got closer and saw that the feathers were moving. Soon she saw a little yellow bill peep out, then another and another. The goose eggs were hatching!

One by one, the shells cracked. Little chirping sounds came from them, and they broke in half to reveal wet new chicks. The little hen was a good mother. She didn't step on any of the tiny goslings as they snuggled under her. Their moist, bedraggled little bodies soon became yellow balls of fluff, with pretty, webbed feet.

Rachel's heart beat faster, and she felt as proud as the little hen herself.

In the next days and weeks, the babies grew quickly. Soon everyone laughed to see the little brown hen strutting along with her family of long-necked geese behind her.

One day Rachel, Emma, Elisabeth, Edna, and Rebecca went down to
the river to play. The sun was warm, and the girls made a wonderful
mudslide. They rubbed themselves with mud, then slid down into the
water, and *splash!* They were clean again, squealing with joy.

Suddenly, the girls noticed a clucking sound, and along the bank came the little brown hen with her family strutting behind. Their long necks were outstretched, and they towered over their little foster mother. When they saw the water, the hen's family charged in, honking, diving, and swimming in delight.

They dipped their bills into the water and splashed water over their backs. The little hen ran frantically back and forth on the shore, clucking loudly. She thought her family was in great danger! They weren't. They were geese and were having a great time in the water.

"Don't worry, little hen," called Rachel. "Your family won't drown! They'll soon be back."

Sure enough, one by one, the geese climbed out onto the bank again, and their nervous little mother led them home.

The girls told the story to their families. They were still laughing about the poor little hen when they went to bed that night.

The little brown hen's children grew bigger and bigger. Soon she didn't pay so much attention to them. She let them search for food for themselves and wander farther away.

Uncle Paul had warned Rachel to keep her geese away from the colony garden. But when she came home one day, she looked in dismay at her own little flower garden. The geese had eaten the flowers and the leaves off her sweet peas, leaving only green stems twisted around the strings.

"You'll have to say good-bye to those geese soon," warned Mueter, "and let them join Uncle Joe's big flock at the edge of the colony."

"But they like to be around the *Hof*, and they'll miss me if I don't feed them," said Rachel.

"They're going to get into trouble," said Mueter, "and then you'll be sorry."

Rachel didn't want to listen to Mueter's warning. She told herself, "I'll watch my geese so well that they *can't* get into trouble." But one day a terrible thing happened. Rachel just couldn't believe it! She ran to the house and burst in the door, sobbing.

"Help! My geese! Something happened to them!" she cried.

Mueter and some of Rachel's brothers and sisters came running, and followed her anxiously out to the yard. There lay Rachel's geese, on their backs with their feet in the air.

"They're *dead!*" wailed Rachel.

"What killed them?" asked her older sister, Sarah. The family stared down at the poor, silent geese.

"Must've been a weasel," said David.

"They bite and suck blood," John added.

Mueter gave him a look. "Hush!" she said. "Rachel, we can use the feathers to make new pillows."

"They could be our present for Cousin Sarah's wedding!" cried little Edna.

It was true. At least something good could come from her poor geese. But nothing could comfort Rachel. She sobbed bitterly.

John picked up the geese by their legs and carried them to the barn. There, Mueter and Aunt Susie plucked the fluffy down off the birds' breasts. They were glad for the extra feathers.

When the birds were stripped, the boys threw them on a pile outside to be hauled away in the morning. The family went back to the house with a sackful of feathers to give Aunt Rachel. She would make pillows for Sarah and for Pete, her groom.

Rachel was quiet and sad that evening. All night she tossed and turned in her *Schlofbonk* bed.

The next morning Rachel woke up with a heavy heart, remembering her poor geese. She tried not to cry again, as she slowly got dressed.

In a minute she heard the front door burst open downstairs, and Voter was laughing loudly. *How can anyone be happy today?* she wondered.

"Come and see, Rachel!" Voter called. Rachel hurried downstairs.

"Follow me," Voter said to the whole family, now gathered in the living room. Sarah, John, Dorothy holding Rachel's hand, David, Emma carrying baby Gladys, Edna, Margaret, Carl, Susanna, and Bertha followed him out to the barnyard.

There, near the barn where they had left them yesterday, were Rachel's geese—*alive!* Some were tottering unsteadily on their webbed feet. Others were still lying down, their wings flapping feebly and their breasts and tummies bare of feathers. Everyone laughed with surprise and wonder.

"Do you know where they've been?" chuckled Voter. "They were in the poppy field yesterday afternoon, and they drugged themselves with poppies!"

"They weren't dead after all!" cried Rachel, clapping her hands and laughing.

"But look at their poor, bare tummies," mourned Edna.

"What can we do about it?" Margaret wondered.

"I know what I'll do," said Rachel, thinking out loud. "I'll make little waistcoats for them. Then I'll know which geese are mine when they join Uncle Joe's big flock!"

Everyone laughed, to think of geese with little waistcoats. Then they all went to enjoy a hearty breakfast.

Background

Rachel Maendel grew up in a special place—a Hutterian colony in Canada, where many families lived together on one big farm, sharing their work and play.

Rachel had a large family and many aunts, uncles, and cousins. The warmth and love of her extended family come through in the true stories in this book. The stories show us that it is possible to have a happy childhood with few material things.

Rachel's Hutterite colony had its own school, kitchen, and dining room. Their tradition of working, eating, and worshiping together as one large family goes back to Anabaptist beginnings in Europe, five hundred years ago.

Although much has changed since Rachel was a little girl, many Hutterite colonies still exist in Manitoba, North Dakota, South Dakota, and states farther west.

The Author

Rachel Maendel was born in 1937, to John and Sarah Maendel at the Rosedale Colony in Manitoba, Canada. Fourth in a family of twelve children, she learned from an early age to give her life in service to others. Rachel lives at the Darvell Bruderhof in Robertsbridge, England.

The Illustrator

Hannah Marsden, born in 1946, has lived all of her life in a Bruderhof community. She cares for the elderly and sick and loves teaching children the joys of nature through drawing and painting. She also lives at the Darvell Bruderhof.